The League

"The League"

ISBN No: " 978-93-90416-83-7"
1st Edition
Language – English and Hindi

Flairs and Glairs
Publication House
Regd. Under MSME Act.

Disclaimer

The anthology is entirely a work of fiction. The compiler has done her best to testify the originality of the content of all the authors and checked for possibilities of plagiarism. All the write-ups are unique and published only in this book.

If any plagiarism and/or error is found, it will solely be the responsibility of the co-author, and not the compiler or publisher.

The opinions expressed in the anthology are only of the co-authors and not of the compiler or publisher.

Acknowledgement

First of all, I thank God, for this life, as a human, has been a lesson full of experiences that have moulded me into the person I am today. To destiny, for teaching me lessons that no one else could.

I'd like to thank my parents for their support, without them, I'd be nothing. My sibling, my love, Nishita Ninave, for her help, support and the blessing she is in my life.

I pay gratitude to my friends Avnish Kumar, Alolika Ray, Momo, Pavan Sharma, Ankita Kumar, and Anandhini Iyappan. You people are not just my friends but are my guiding angels who I know I can blindly rely upon.

Shubham Shah and the entire team of Flairs and Glairs, I salute your dedication and helping nature. You are the reason why the book was possible.

Last but not the least, all the co-authors who were extremely cooperative throughout the project. You all are the whole and soul of the book. All I wish is health and happiness for you all!

Co Authors

1. Shubham Shah (Founder, F&G)
2. Ishani Agarwal (Co Founder F and G)
3. Grishma Ninave (Compiler)
4. Ishika Agarwal
5. Reema Ninawe
6. Trisha Banerjee
7. Ankita
8. Avnish Kumar
9. Nawang Chugh
10. Sudhanshu Palandurkar
11. Krishan Kant Sen
12. Faij Ahmad
13. Shivansh Sharma
14. Hinduja Krishnaraj
15. Deepjyoti Chowdhury
16. Shijin Ravi C
17. Somesh Kumar Jha
18. Kalamkaar
19. Ashima Jain
20. Mihir Deshpande
21. Rubal Choudhary
22. Harsh Raju Ninawe
23. Mayuri Valanju
24. D. Agilan
25. Nikhitha Vanga
26. Jude Fernandes
27. Mansha Poddar
28. Vishal Agrawal
29. Harshal Raju Ninawe
30. विनय झा
31. Tushar Bhakte
32. Samiksha Wasudeo Kumbhare
33. Sarabjot Purba

34. Khushbu Rathore
35. Spoorthi H C
36. Jeevitha.S
37. Auqib Hassan
38. Debangsh Das
39. Sumedha Dutt
40. Debanjana Ghatak
41. Sahaj Sabharwal
42. Shivika Sharma
43. Priya Jha
44. Khushi Mohan Kothale
45. Sahina Ghugha
46. Surekha Wankhede
47. Piyush Bhardwaj
48. Karan Vijay Nandanwar
49. Aastha Shukla
50. Ishwari Kishor Shirur
51. Hema Kirthiga J
52. Sarvesh Bagde
53. Mohit Goyal
54. Siddharth Supali

Shubham Shah

(Founder- Flairs and Glairs)

Shubham Shah, entrepreneur at "Flairs & Glairs" a brand with dynamics in events organizing and cultural educational pan INDIA, He is a 26yr. old guy who recently has entered, the digital platform of imprinting emotions. He has initiated with his own open mic platform to help budding poets and aspiring writers under his brand named as "Teekhe Zasbaaat"
He is a commerce graduate from Bhagalpur City of Bihar.
He says Writing has impersonated him since childhood and he has now been writing for over a decade!
Cooking, on the other hand, is his passion! He also mentions, trying out new things just tickles him!
When asked sir, Why SPICY EMOTIONS?

He smiled and added, “agar jasbaat teekhe na ho toh wo jasbaat kaha” Spices are all that blends! So do his words!
As a chef, he presents to you his dish! Hot and freshly served! Taste it! Feel it! Enjoy it! You can also find his writing in the Solo book “Teekhe Zasbaaat” and 70+ anthologies. With his passion to explore opportunities across Platforms he is working with keen devotion and We wish him all the very best for his future ventures
Share your reviews on his

INSTAGRAM

@spicy_emotions
@shubham4shah

Or via email on

shubham2shah@gmail.com

To stay tuned to his work and opportunities follow his business Handles

INSTAGRAM FACEBOOK YOUTUBE

@flairsandglairs
@teekhezasbaaat

WEBSITE:

https://flairsandglairs.in/
https://flairsandglairs.com/

Ishani Agarwal

(Co Founder- Flairs and Glairs)

Ishani Agarwal
Born and brought up in Kolkata, she has done her schooling and college from here itself. She is doing her post-graduation at the moment. Ishani loves talking to people around, and is excited for this new beginning of hers! Been a Compiler for 35+ Anthologies, and in the process for more, also, co-authored in 100+ Anthologies, Ishani is very Happy with how her life is turning out now!
Insta handle: Ishani_agarwal_quotes

Grishma Ninave
(Compiler)

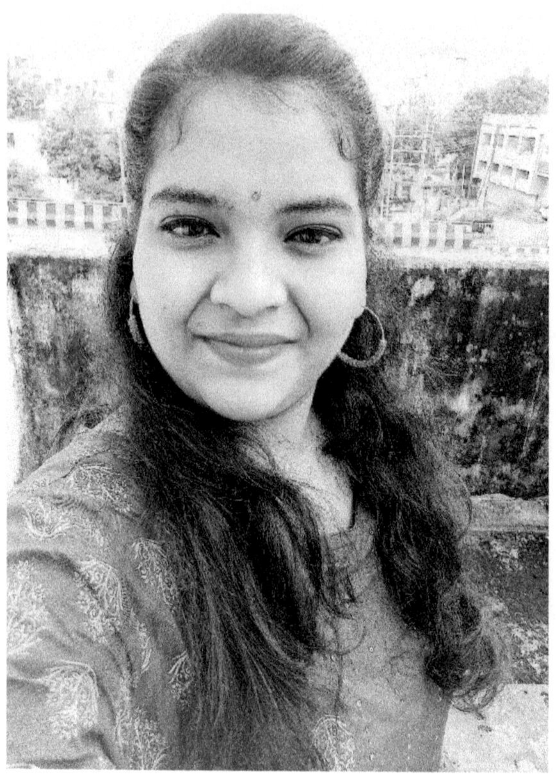

A student of science and an admirer of arts from Nagpur, Maharashtra.
Currently working as a Project Head at Flairs and Glairs Publication House.
A minion millennial with extra-large dreams.
Is in an active rebellion with her mother about the number of books she must have in the house. When not reading, can be found writing and reviewing books a lot.

A firm believer that music is what can revive and reconcile the world. She's one of those people who love greys more than colours and she's like colourful autumn too at the same time.
Admires old school love stories and retro music.
A Capricorn girl who believes hearts are more important than physical appearances. Is into deep talks with a very few people, but believes they are the driving force of joy in her life. Loves travelling to places where there are mountains, trees, hills and treks.
No wonder nature's beauty strikes a chord within her.
The guiding light in her life is the quote, "Don't search for happiness, because it's not something you find, it's something you create!"

Has participated more than 95 anthologies and Compiled the Titles – Whispers of the Pen, Ansuni Aawaaz, Monika, Dil Ki Dastaan, Sizzling Thoughts and working on more.

E-mail – ninavegrishma@gmail.com
Instagram - @grish_ninave; @the_compiled_words

Dearest Captain Cool

The aura created after a helicopter shot in the world cup, is something I will always remember.

You are someone like us, yet one of a kind. Indeed, everyone is a "*pal do pal ka shayar*", but a very few can maintain their "*hasti* and *rawani*" even after signing off. You, my captain cool, are a saga I will always cherish. To people, you might be just a chapter who occupied a limited space in the book called cricket, but to me, you are those pages which I will never be tired of reading. In those pages, sometimes my lips will curve into a smile, and sometimes I'll drench the pages with my tears, but what will remain constant will be my love for you.

The respect I carry for you is what radiates from you when you are around people; irrespective of who they are.

You are an inspiration,

The epitome calmness,

But above all,

You are a lesson, of how a little thing can turn into something great just by hard work and dedication.

Ishika Agarwal

Ishika is a 16 years old girl.
Writing for her is nothing else but a passion. She hails from the city of Joy and Art. She has been a Co-author in 30+ anthologies in the recent past, all adding on experiences to her. Been a part of India book of Record projects like Black and World Record projects like 15 wonders of Poetry, Ishika is paving her way to success.

(1)

Why should boys have all the privileges?

Why should they have all the rights?

Why should girls be in control rather than boys?

My main question is WHY. I am a girl but I want to live my life like every boy can live.

I wanna go on solo trips.

I wanna go clubbing.

I wanna party.

I wanna ride a bike.

But everyone asks me "what will people say?"

I say I don't are.

I wanna live my life like anybody else and I will live my life my way!

Reema Ninawe

Reema is a biotechnologist. She is a student who dreams to live her dreams at the fullest. She lives in Chennai and her native is Nagpur. Reema is a mixture of Maharashtrian tadka with south Indian accent. She has good poetic skills and believes that writing gives her a relief from everything. She writes in different languages like Hindi, English, Tamil, Marathi.

And it all began in April 23, 2008. The scorching sun felt like cheering for our team with all love and vividness of the colour. Between chasing the *Parasakthi* express train and not trying to blink our eyes to the exquisite arrow's run out.

Whenever the name is pronounced, goosebump is a huge compliment.

From the highest run-scorer for our team and the most charming one from the beginning to tweeting *Thirukkural* and sharing love to everyone. We fall but will roar back thunderously.

From dancing to the champion's beat to lifting our heads up to capture the helicopter.

All the shouts, noise, whistles and the cheering turned out to be our new anthem. Everything felt like home permeated with Yellow

Winning or losing doesn't matter when it comes to family. We are the Yellow Army and we love CSK. It felt like everyone around me were celebrating a grand festival. I have never been so overwhelmed. I danced to the rhythm. I screamed the throat out of me. I never felt so happy. Everyone in the vicinity was of the same colour with no discrimination of what complex they were. Everyone had the same flag no matter from where they hail. Everyone sang to the same chorus no matter what was their anthem to live. Everyone danced as if they knew each other. Everyone celebrated. Everyone hugged. Tears rolled upon everyone's cheeks each time they won.

Trisha Banerjee

Trisha Banerjee, born in the city of joy, Kolkata, is as happy hearted, friendly and with positive vibes just like the city itself. A young writer who spends her time with books and nature. She is adventurous and challenges herself with something new every day.

IPL era is the era where the tv's, mobiles, computers are worshipped so that the Indians can watch the IPL match uninterrupted. The favourite sport of India is watched by all Indians of the country and why not it is too interesting to watch. People wait for months before the announcement and commencement of the league is made. Their adrenaline-rush is high since the announcement itself. Amidst the lockdown, cricket league is one of the boosters to people. The people have something to keep themselves engaged after a lot of pressure. Indian have always been fans of cricket since time immemorial. Cricket is not just a match series for Indians, it is an emotion for Indians. An emotion which the Indians cannot deny. We, being proud cricket lovers, sit at our favourite spots with some popcorns, pakoras, chips, tea, cold drink, coffee etc. before the time and wait for the match to begin even though we know its not time yet. During the match, we are so engrossed in watching every moment of the players that nothing seems more important than the match. Wasting even one second seems like an hour. Cheering for our favourite team and player has to be the most thing even though we are not in the stadium. A "six", "four" and an out set not only the stadium but the entire country into the roar and its effect can be heard in every corner of the country. Every city supporting its favourite team, dancing in their victory, mourning over their loss but never giving up hope and support. The spirit and love for cricket will never diminish from the heart of the Indians.

Ankita

Ankita was raised in the Coal Capital of India, Dhanbad. She is an ambivert. She is a travel freak and is truly a foodie. She has a fetish for novels who loves the idea of buying books concerning genres of Suspense thriller, Murder Mystery, Inspirational. The best escape for her is sketching and listening to music.

The Yellow Jersey

From roaring Bleed Blue to Whistle Podu, we fans have done it all for Cricket, but most importantly for our very own Jharkhandi guy who chased towards his dreams and brought all possible laurels for our country. Even the history of his successive wins knows it well that a star like Mahi with such magnificence and magnanimity will never be born again and the history will never be repeated.

The colour yellow which once resonated with sunshine and everything bright now holds the reflection a team that is led by Mahi and backed by hundreds of fans, most of those having no internal connection nor attachment with Chennai but Thala is all we recite for the whole of the IPL season, you see. The sixes and fours, the team discussion led by Dhoni before starting of every match, the wicket-keeping, the winning moment and taking away a wicket as a souvenir, we fans live and yearn for these pocketful of happiness. May you keep hitting helicopter shots and may we keep witnessing them all.

Avnish Kumar

A resolute recluse, Avnish is an anachronistic soul.
He is a voracious reader, aspiring author and has a momentous dream of owning as many books as humanly possible.
A chemistry teacher professionally, he lives his life through his other hobbies of writing, music, bhangra and avoiding as many social gatherings as possible.
He is also fond of rhymes and loves reading and writing shayaris. He has an immaculate love for learning new languages and is currently on his way to explore Urdu.

Cricket - Through the lens of India

To a layman, any sport can be defined as an activity that induces and enhances physical and mental dexterity while providing enjoyment to both the players as well as spectators. One can define cricket the same way all around the world. But not in India.

Post-Independence, a multitude of forces - both internal and external proved divisive for the people of India. Amidst political turmoil, wars and regional differences, there were very few factors that bonded the people of this vast country together.

And as if on cue, in 1983, Kapil Dev and his men started winning matches in the World Cup in England by beating teams that had bigger statures than India in the world of cricket. It was the ultimate underdog story. And on every match day, the country united in tuning their transistors and radios to the correct frequency to hear the commentary of India's matches. Metaphorically, if the communities of India were different fabrics then Cricket became the thread that stitched us together. And since then, cricket has remained that. Today, when in the middle of the day, hordes gather at a Pan shop whether in a city or a remote village, you know that it is a match day for Team India.

Cricket is a religion in India, because it does what a bonafide religion couldn't do but was supposed to - it unites Indian people even on their worst days. And the great Sachin Tendulkar is hailed a God not because of his exceptional skill and impeccable talent, but because when he batted against the fiercest oppositions, he made a balloon seller standing roadside in Varanasi feel the same joy as a suited-up businessman in Bangalore. He united the people of India in their emotions.

A sport that is more galvanizing than dissecting in its essence is ought to be special for emotional people like us. We may not be Devaki to cricket but we are it's Yashoda. And cricket to us will always be the chirpy, charismatic and beloved Kanha.

'In India, superstitions are sacred, cricketers are icons and cricket itself is a faith.'.

Nawang Chugh

Nawang considers himself as not so very positive person, but is trying hard to change himself. He is very thoughtful and this is why he loves poetry. He believes that writing is one of the most beautiful things that god has given to us because whatever you will write next has never been written. Cheers!

सचिन! तेरा शुक्रिया...

बात थी कुछ 1989 की। जब एक महान खिलाड़ी ने मैदान पर कदम रखा। सामने थी पाकिस्तान की मज़बूत टीम जिसमे वसीम, वक़ार जैसे दिग्गज गेंदबाज़ भरे थे। मगर 16 साल का ये नौजवान कहाँ हार मानने वाला था? हालांकि अपनी पहली पारी में सिर्फ 15 रन ही बना पाए थे सचिन पर उनका खेलने का अंदाज़ लोग उस दिन देख चुके थे।

1993 में मेरा जन्म हुआ। क्रिकेट खेलना जैसे मेरी रागों में था और क्रिकेट देखना मेरा सबसे बड़ा शौंक। मुझे आज भी याद है जब 1999 में मैंने क्रिकेट देखना शुरू किया तो सबसे पहला नाम मेरी ज़बान पर सचिन तेंदुलकर का आया और तब से वे मेरे पसंदीदा खिलाड़ी बन गए। मुझे एक बात का हमेशा दुख रहेगा कि आज भी मैं उनकी सबसे सर्वश्रेष्ठ पारी जो कि 1998 में ऑस्ट्रेलिया के ख़िलाफ़ शारजाह में खेली गई थी, वो मैं लाइव नही देख सका। पर जब से उन्हें देखना शुरू किया था तब से मेरे लिए क्रिकेट का मतलब सिर्फ सचिन ही था।

सीधे बल्ले से उनके वो शॉट मेरे लिए उतने ही खास हैं जितना कि एक इंसान के लिए अपना परिवार। उनकी हर एक अच्छी पारी पूरे भारत को खुश कर देती थी। अपनी फिल्म में उन्होंने वो हर लम्हा दिखाया जो मैं कभी नहीं भूलूँगा।

2003 विश्व कप के फाइनल में भारत की हार बर्दाश्त करना सबके लिए बहुत मुश्किल था मगर जब मैंने सचिन को रोते हुए देखा तब मेरे भी आंसू आ गए। बस एक ट्रॉफी ही तो है मगर उस क्रिकेटर को सिर्फ वो ही चाहिए थी। अपनी ताबड़तोड़ बल्लेबाज़ी से मास्टर

ब्लास्टर ने भारत को अनेक ट्रॉफी जितायी मगर विश्व कप का सपना अभी बाकी था।

2011 में वानखेड़े स्टेडियम में जब धोनी ने वो छक्का लगाया तब सचिन की वो खुशी मैं कभी नही भूल सकता। उनके हाथ में विश्व कप था और उनके अंदर वो 16 साल के बच्चे जैसा जोश। बाद में सामने आया कि वे पूरी रात अपने कमरे में पार्टी करते रहे क्योंकि बरसों बाद उनका सपना पूरा हुआ।

मैं नहीं मानता कि सचिन एक भगवान की तरह है पर फिर ये सोचता हूँ कि जो इंसान हर किसी को खुश कर देता था, वो भगवान से कम तो नहीं है।

थैंक यू सचिन...

Sudhanshu Palandurkar

Sudhanshu Palandurkar belongs from Nagpur. He has an education in General science and keen interest with background loaded with marketing and graphic design projects, centred around modernizing consumer experience. His love for nature and travel is die hard and he is planning to take retirement from his career within 40's. Happy soul would describe more effective about him.

Indian Premier League

The concept of premier league was initiated by Lalit Modi who was the chairman of IPL. Cricket and its association with the Indian emotions is large on the faces of the common mass. People religiously worship cricket and this trend has been going on for years now. It is definitely more than just a game, where the cricketers are regarded as demigods and factually worshipped by the common man. The newest form of cricket, the Twenty20 format has of late created history in the arena of sports. After this new cricket format was introduced, people have gained more interest and thus the popularity graph is only going up, It is the most successful business in the world now days because cricket is the most redound and loving game and it has won the heart of always everybody. Its again an ultra-mode for gambling too, India bet, bet365 are some of the applications which again destroying youths.

Krishan Kant Sen

कहानियों से कहानी का सृजन करने वाले "कृष्ण कान्त सेन", राजस्थान के छोटे से शहर बाराँ से आते है। उनकी रचनायें अंग्रेजी व हिन्दी, दोनो भाषाओं में मिलती हैं। सगुण भक्ति धारा को आदर्श मानने वाले "कृष्ण कान्त" की काव्य रचनाओं में माधुर्य व ओज का विशेष प्रभाव है।

उपन्यास पढ़ने के शौकीन "कृष्ण कान्त", वर्तमान मैं अंग्रेजी भाषा से उच्च शिक्षा में अध्ययनरत हैं।

साथ ही लेखन के अतिरिक्त फोटोग्राफी में भी विशेष रुचि रखते हैं।

वर्ष था 2007 का, भारतीय क्रिकेट टीम बुरी तरह हार कर विश्व कप से बाहर हो चुकी थी। खिलाड़ियों पर लगातार सवाल उठ रहे थे। सवाल उठना भी लाज़िमी था। 2003 विश्व कप में फाइनल में पहुँचने वाली टीम का 2007 में जो हाल हुआ, वह किसी भी तरह से सहानुभूति लायक नही रह गया था। टीम ने हर क्षेत्र में निराश किया।

निराशा को टालने व एक नयी कोर टीम खड़ी करने एवं नयी प्रतिभाओं को सामने लाना अभी भी एक चुनौती थी। इन सब के बीच पूर्व भारतीय कप्तान कपिल देव एवं उनके कुछ साथी कुछ अलग करने की सोच रहे थे। अन्तरराष्ट्रीय स्तर पर चलने वाले क्लब फुटबाल को देखते हुए वे क्रिकेट क्लब का एक नया प्रारूप लाना चाह रहे थे। इसी को देखते हुए उन्होने इंडियन क्रिकेट लीग लाँच कर दी।

इंडियन क्रिकेट लीग, भारत में एक नयी शुरुआत थी। जिसकी सफलता का कोई अंदाजा नही था। देखते ही देखते भारत, पाकिस्तान एवं बांग्लादेश में ही 9 क्लब तैयार कर दिये गये। (मुम्बई चैम्प्स, चेन्नई सुपरस्टार्स, चंडीगढ़ लॉयन्स, हैदराबाद हीरोज, रॉयल बंगाल टाइगर्स, दिल्ली जियांट्स, अहमदाबाद रॉकेट्स, लाहौर बादशाह, ढाका वारियर्स)। ये सभी क्लब निजी संस्थाओं से संबद्ध थे। इन क्लब के साथ ही तीनों देश की एक-एक कोर टीम भी बना दी गई; साथ ही एक विश्व एकादश की भी कोर टीम बना ली गई। पहला सीजन नवंबर 2007 से प्रस्तावित था। क्लब की प्रस्तावना के विषय में बीसीसीआई को जब तक अवगत कराया जाता, तब तक बीसीसीआई एवं आईसीएल समिति के बीच मतभेद खुलकर सामने आ गया। परिणाम यह रहा की कपिल देव को नेशनल क्रिकेट एकेडमी से हटा दिया गया। अन्तरराष्ट्रीय क्रिकेट परिषद ने भी इसे मंजूरी देने से यह कहकर इनकार कर दिया कि पहले बीसीसीआई से मामला सुलझाया जाये। बीसीसीआई ने साफ आदेश जारी कर दिया कि जो भी आईसीएल में खेलेगा, उसे बीसीसीआई द्वारा आजीवन प्रतिबंधित किया जायेगा। इस कारण कई बड़े नाम लीग से जुड़ने से रह गये बहरहाल विवादों के बीच इसका पहला सीजन शुरु हो चुका था, लेकिन विवाद थमने का नाम नही ले रहे थे। बीसीसीआई से संबद्ध स्टेडियम ने भी मना कर दिया। इस कारण रेलवे से संबद्ध स्टेडियम में इसका आयोजन कराया गया। बड़े नाम नदारद रहने से यह लीग लोकप्रिय नही हो सकी। असफलता के बाद भी इसका आयोजन किया जा रहा था। लेकिन खिलाड़ी आशंकित थे कि कहीं उनका

करियर यही ना खत्म हो जाये। ऐसे में और भी खिलाड़ी इसे छोड़ रहे थे। यह लीग एक कमजोर लीग बनकर रह गयी। इस लीग की प्रतिस्पर्धा में बीसीसीआई ने भी अपनी लीग की घोषणा कर दी, जिसमें प्राइज मनी भी बहुत अधिक कर दी गयी। नाम रखा गया आईपीएल अर्थात् इण्डियन प्रीमीयर लीग। आईपीएल की घोषणा होते ही कई बड़े नाम इससे जुड़ते चले गये। बीसीसीआई समर्थित होने से करियर की भी किसी को चिंता नही थी, साथ ही बहुत बड़ी धनराशि का निवेश था, जो हर किसी को आकर्षित कर सकता था। किसी भी खिलाड़ी को इतना तो मिलना तय था कि वो उसके पूरे वर्ष के लिए पर्याप्त था। साथ ही बड़ी हस्तियाँ शुमार होने से सफलता भी सुनिश्चित प्रतीत हो रही थी। स्पॉन्सर के रूप में डीएलएफ ने भी बहुत बड़ा निवेश किया था। प्रथम सत्र के आयोजन के लिए आठ टीमों को प्रस्तावित किया।(मोहाली, दिल्ली, मुम्बई, जयपुर, हैदराबाद, बेंगलूरु, कोलकाता और चेन्नई)। जिनमे हर टीम को एक बड़ा खिलाड़ी कोर सदस्य के रूप में उपलब्ध करवा दिया। चैन्नई टीम को ऐसा कोर सदस्य नही मिल पाया। बारी थी खिलाड़ियों की नीलामी की, तो विदेशी खिलाड़ी भी शामिल हो गये। विश्व स्तर के बड़े बड़े नामों के बीच घरेलु खिलाड़ियों को भी अच्छी रकम मिलना तय था। पहले सत्र की नीलामी में महेन्द्र सिंह धोनी की सबसे बड़ी बोली लगी। उन्हे चेन्नई की फ्रेंचाइजी ने 6 करोड़ की भारी भरकम कीमत पर खरीदा और कप्तान नियुक्त कर दिया।

18 अप्रेल 2008 को पहला मैच हुआ कोलकाता और बेंगलूरू के बीच। कोलकाता की ओर से मेक्कुलम ने पहले ही मैच में शतक जड़ दिया और बेंगलूरू को 140 रन से बड़ी हार का सामना करना पड़ा। पहले सीजन में कागजों पर सबसे कमजोर टीम जयपुर की राजस्थान रॉयल्स नजर आ रही थी, लेकिन टीम जयपुर में अपना एक भी मैच नही हारी और पहले ही सीजन का खिताब चेन्नई सुपरकिंग्स को फाइनल में हराकर अपने नाम किया। पहले सीजन में शॉन मार्श(किंग्स इलेवन पंजाब) नें सर्वाधिक 616 रन बनाये और राजस्थान रॉयल्स के सुहैल तनवीर ने 22 विकेट चटकाये। शेन वाटसन को प्लेयर ऑफ द टूर्नामेंट चुना गया।

इस प्रकार शुरू हुआ आईपीएल कई उतार चढ़ाव के साथ साल दर साल परवान चढ़ता गया। स्पॉन्सर भी बदले लेकिन जोश कम नही हुआ। चुनावों के कारण इसे दक्षिण अफ्रीका और संयुक्त अरब अमीरात में भी इसका आयोजन हुआ। फिक्सिंग के दाग भी लगे, लेकिन यह लीग फिर भी परवान

चढ़ती गयी। चेन्नई सुपरकिंग्स हर बार प्लेऑफ में पहुँची, तो मुम्बई इंडियन्स नें सर्वाधिक बार खिताब अपने नाम किया। कुछ टीमे पीछे छूट गयी तो कुछ नयी जुड़ गयी, लेकिन इसका प्रभाव कम नही हुआ। यह क्रिकेट की दुनिया में विश्व की सबसे बड़ी लीग बन गई। आज भी यह उत्तरोत्तर वृद्धि करती ही जा रही है, और आशा करते हैं, आगे भी अनवरत जारी रहेगी।

Faij Ahmad

He is trainee navigational officer cadet at shipping corporation of india under ministry of shipping, Govt of India. He is free-lance writer.
A proud sainikian.

Where Talents Meet Opportunity

League of 20 overs each
Festival of India
Band with same note shouts
"Indian Premier league"
Tune resonating in ears
Vibes in cool decency
Flows in river of courtesy

Zeal of competency
In between fans
Roaring bloods
In mood of fantasy
Fighting with each other
With spirit of camaraderie
For a trophy

Eyes sharp on television
Eyelid up every time
Watching ball to ball
Waiting winning streak
Heart high throbbing
On ounce of every ball
Talents playing on "peak of the hat"

Shivansh Sharma

He is Shivansh Sharma. Basically from Indore but pursuing MBA (Marketing & Hr) in Mysore Karnataka. He always has passion towards writing the thoughts which comes in to his mind. A hardcore foodie as he belongs to Indore. He is the one who is always ready to help to his near ones. His life revolves around his family and friends. He is always self-motivated, enthusiastic and person with positive vibes. He is co-author of 10+ books and compiler of 1 book. His only belief is just live happily and enjoy every moment of life.
You can contact him on IG @shivanshrockzzzzz

धोनी

आईपीएल के किंग हो,
सुपर किंग्स के सरताज हो,
सबसे ज्यादा पसंद है
हमे तुम्हरा अंदाज़,
हर वक़्त बस तुम्हे देखने को
दिल है चाहता हर बार,
हर बार अनहोनी को
होनी करने का है तुम्हरा काम,
कुछ वक़्त में बाजी पलट दे,
वो है धोनी की निशानी,
शांत रहना तुमसे है सीखा,
इसलिए कहते है कैप्टन कूल,
सी एस के में नाम है कमाया,
सारे काटें बन गए फूल,
3 बार चैंपियन है बने इस खेल के
कभी ना हिम्मत हारी तुमने,
जब भी धोनी मेरे छक्के,
नाचते नाचते देखे सब फैंन,
सी एस के की जान हो तुम,
भले ही बदले जमाना,
सी एस के है नभ का सूरज,
बाकी लगे सितारे,
बाकी सब है डरते,
जब तुम मैदान में आते,
तुम हो वो जिससे हर बॉलर है डरता
फिर भी सबके चहिते हो,
क्योंकि सबके जुबान पर बस नाम धोनी है।

Hinduja Krishnaraj

She was a budding writer, who love to pour all the feelings and emotions, in one type, that is writing. She is also a co-author of five books.

Colours Of Love

There are many colours of love,
And, I love to choose you.
You are the one, who made me love cricket;
You are the one, where everyone celebrates from their heart:
You are the one, who is the pride for our state;
You are the one, which made everyone to mingle with emotions;
You are the one, what everyone is waiting for;
You are the one, that surveys all the thunders;
You are the one, who will be always in our thoughts;
You are the one, which is giving many fans love;
You are the one, colour which is not mixed with others;
You are the one, to proudly say, my yellow love, CSK.

Deepjyoti Chowdhury

Deepjyoti Chowdhury embraces reading and writing as her escape from the real world as well as a window to it. She is a strong believer of Christ and Karma. Written in 100+ anthologies, she is the author of "Heartfelt musings" and "The staircase to freedom". Her main aim is to heal people and make them smile through her art of writing. You can follow her on Instagram at dj_writes_to_heal .

Cricket

The blissful moment when I discovered,
That watching cricket I secretly preferred.

Being from a school where Dhoni had studied,
Where pride and amaze the students bleed.

The Captain had always made me proud,
And removed every questioning doubt.

Being from a small town was now a bliss,
As great heights can be achieved with practice.

Ranchi is now known to all nation,
Because of a single soul full of passion.

Cricket and IPL I no longer miss,
As watching my star fills my heart with bliss.

Shijin Ravi C

He is Mr Shijin Ravi C from Kerala. He is pursuing BSc Hons Agriculture graduate. He is a young poet and co-author of many anthologies today. Some of his anthologies are 'The golden words', 'The uncertain periods', 'My success ladder', 'Safar', 'Her voice', 'Positive vibes' etc.
His mail ID is shijinravi23@gmail.com.
His Instagram ID is stolen.pearl .

Right Ball Right Shot

With a ball and bat, it begins to run,
With the crowds on feet to cheer and tweet,
It's the match between two real teams,
Both for wins with all their skills.

Players get ready assembly on the said,
Just ball by ball it goes on to score,
With a bad and good ball hit too fast,
Sometimes a six or an out to cheer.

Everyone is so quick from ball to bat,
The field set to smear the ropes aiming to tear,
That it may be a bowler or a batsman's gear,
With all that prays to unite the gadgets to fire.

The game is cool with wide and no-ball.
Even fun with six and fours all over,
So unlucky is you are caught or bowled,
Being worst is a duck or hit wicket.

But as all know game speeds with eleven,
All different to watch and in approach,
Making it taste so higher than near,
The best part is the umpires call to hire.

Somesh Kumar Jha

Pursuing B.Tech in Electrical Domain from Gautam Buddha University, Greater Noida, Delhi NCR.

"Having a goal isn't enough to succeed, but you have to be smart enough so that you win, where the chances of your success are quite low".

Love for IPL

Once i asked someone what do you get after watching IPL for hours and hours...
He smiled and answered me politely.

IPL isn't Indian premier league,
But it's Indians playing lovingly.
Maybe Catching the ball doesn't let you win the match but you win thousands of hearts.
IPL isn't just a game but it's an emotion,
Sometimes we win we lose.
For us, cricket Isn't just a game,
But it's one of the biggest Indian festivals.
We live we cheer we celebrate it with our loved ones.

Kalamkaar

This is Kalamkaar. He is from Uttarakhand but brought up in Meerut (UP). His hobbies are reading and writing. He loves writing. He is part of 210+ Anthologies as Co-Author. Won 150+ certificates in writing. He is simple and people observer.

एम एस धोनी

रांची का एक मध्य वर्ग का लड़का
खेलता था फुटबॉल और था गोलकीपर
बाइक का वो दीवाना था
दिया क्रिकेट के कोच सर ने चांस उसको तब बना वो विकेटकीपर
आने के लिए क्रिकेट मे लगाई अपनी रेलवे की नौकरी दाव पर
आया फिर क्रिकेट की दुनिया मे नया सितारा
क्रिकेट फिर लगा उसको सबसे प्यारा था, खेलने दोस्तों के संग जाता था
चलता बल्ला उसका सबसे न्यारा
शार्ट वो ऐसे खेलता बॉलर भी डरजाते
डाले कोनसी बोल उसको पूछने कप्तान के पासजाते
डाले अगर योर्कर तो हेलीकाप्टर शार्ट घूमजाता
बॉल फिर सीदा आसमान को चूम के आता
बुरी परिस्थिति मे भी करता नहीं था कोई भी भूल,कहते थे उसको कप्तान कूल
क्रिकेट का वो है नायब सितारा, जिसकी वजा से टी 20 और विशव कप हुआ था हमारा
दिलाये कही ख़िताब उसने करा परचम भारत का ऊपर
अनहोनी को भी जो होनी कर देता था
नाम था उसका एम एस धोनी

Ashima Jain

She is passionate about her work. She is honest and loves to accept new challenges. She is loyal. She knows cooking dancing etc. She is open-hearted and open-minded.

आईपीएल

ये खेल नही एक त्यौहार है,
पूरा भारत करता इसका इंतज़ार है!
माहौल भी बनाते ऐसा की दुनिया मे
लोग इसके आने का करते इंतज़ार है
सट्टेबाज भी इसमे खूब कमाते है
हर गेंद पे अंपायर अपना कमाल दिखाते है
आठ टीमें भी इसमे टकराती है
पर हमेशा आर.सी.बी सबका दिल जीत जाती है
सी .एस.के की टीम भी खतरनाक बन जाती है
हर टीम में वो अपना खौफ बनाती है
अस.आर.एच् की टीम ने भी कमाल दिखाया है,
वार्नर के दम पे ईतिहास है,
पंजाब की टीम के क्या कहने जनाब,,
गेल के दम अपनी उम्मीद जागती है,
बौलिंग में सबसे ज़्यादा रन वही खाती हैं,
के .के.आर की टीम का भी अलग जलवा है,,
रसेल के दम पे बोलता इनका बल्ला है,
दिल्ली की टीम भी बड़ी खयाली है,
रबाडा की गेंदबाजी अच्छे अच्छों पर भारी है,
सुपर ओवर में वो अपना कमाल दिखाता है,
सारे बल्लेबाज़ों के आखो में आंसू लाता है,
तो यही है पूरे आईपीएल की कहानी एक,,,
छोटी सी जुबानी.

Mihir Deshpande

True Cricket Fan

क्रिकेट

नाम सूनकरही पुरी ऊर्जा हमारे अंदर आ जाती हैं!!
ये सिर्फ खेल नही एक त्योहार है.भारत मै तो हर एक घर मै क्रिकेट का नशा होता ही है! यह खेल ही ऐसा है की हमारी भावना इस खेलसे जुडी हुई है! हमारा सारा बचपन क्रिकेट ने तो खूबसुरत बनाया है! क्रिकेट खेलते खेलते हूए तो हम बडे हुए है! क्रिकेट ने हमे खेल भावना क्या होती है वो सिखाया,हमे तंदुरुस्त रहना सिखाया. क्रिकेट ने हमारी दोस्ती मजबुत की,एकता का पाठ भी पढाया. उमीद रखना सिखाया,संयम क्या होता यह सिखाया,और बहोत कुछ सिखाया!! पता नही अभीभी हर एक मिडल क्लास मा-बाप को क्रिकेटसे नफरत क्यो होती है!!

क्रिकेट की बहोत प्रसिद्ध लीग है IPL! हर एक क्रिकेट प्रेमी केलीये IPL मतलब सोने पे सुहागा ऐसा होता है! हर एक मॅच रोमांच से भरा हुवा होता है.हर एक टीम एक से बढकर एक होती है!नजाने IPL की वजाह सें कितने लोगो को रोजगार मिला,अच्छा मंच मिला, अच्छा वातावरण मिला,आगे जाकर यही लोग भारत का प्रतिनिधित्व करने लगे!!कुछ अलग ही मिझाझ है IPL का!! हर एक को खुशी बाटता है यह क्रिकेट का त्योहार!!

द इनक्रेडिबल प्रीमियर लीग ॥

Rubal Choudhary

This is Rubal Choudhary from Gurgaon, Haryana. She is 20-year-old and currently pursuing English Hons. from Delhi University. She aspires to become an IAS officer. She is an Anthology head at BookSquirrel.

Other than this she has co-authored 50+ Anthologies, and has Compiled 18 books in which one had won and recognized by India book of records- BLACK. Earlier, the writing was not a cup of tea for her but later she realised that she can write too. She believes write until it suits as natural as to respire.

Great leaders never tend to fail. For them, opposition is another opposition. That is what our legend MAHI is.

Harsh Raju Ninawe

He is studying at Shri Shivaji Science College, Nagpur.
His hobbies are bike riding, playing cricket, cooking, playing badminton etc.

एक अविस्मरणीय खेळ ''क्रिकेट''

क्रिकेट : एक लोकप्रिय सांघिक खेळ. हा इंग्लंडचा राष्ट्रीय खेळ असून तो इंग्लंडप्रमाणेच भारत, ऑस्ट्रेलिया, दक्षिण आफ्रिका, वेस्ट इंडीज, पाकिस्तान व न्यूझीलंड ह्या राष्ट्रकुलातील देशांतही लोकप्रिय आहे. ह्या सात देशांमध्ये क्रिकेटचे अधिकृत कसोटी सामने होतात.

खेळाची लोकप्रियता व महत्त्व : क्रिकेटचा खेळ हा बराचसा बेभरवशाच्या स्वरूपाचा आहे. कित्येकदा भरवशाचे फलंदाज एकामागून एक पटापट बाद होतात, तर अनपेक्षितपणे काही फलंदाज धावसंख्या वाढवत नेतात. गोलंदाजाच्या बाबतीतही ह्याच अनिश्चिततेचा अनुभव येतो. ह्या अद्‌भुतरम्य अनिश्चिततेमुळे या खेळास विलक्षण लोकप्रियता लाभली आहे.

आयुष्यात घडणाऱ्या अनेक घटनांसाठी जणू क्रिकेट आपल्याला तयार करते. क्रिकेटमुळे समजते की यश -अपयश हे दोन्ही किती क्षणभंगुर असते. निराशा किंवा आशा या दोन्ही गोष्टी सारख्याच बिनमहत्तवाच्या आहेत. कोणताही खेळ का असेना हार किंवा जित होणेच आहे. जसे नाण्यांचे दोन बाजू असतात त्याप्रकारे खेळामध्ये पण हार किंवा जित होतच असते.

Mayuri Valanju

Mayuri Valanju, resident of Mumbai. She is commerce mastered pursuing higher education. Social Media Manager of Fanatixx and Anthology Department Head of Spectrum of Thoughts Publication, an affiliate of FanatiXx. Co-author of many anthologies. Her debut book was 'Spectrum of Thoughts'. Writing is Peace for her. She is an addict of Korean, Turkish and Chinese dramas. Coffee is her love and sound of book pages flipping like her the most. Connecting with people and talking to them is what she loves.
You can find her on Instagram @scribblers_abode.
Also can contact for business info over: - 9136233773

She Cheered aloud; it was a run-out.
He huffed and puffed rolling his sleeves up.
Faf was on the strike, balled by the handsome tiger; Pollard.
She mimicked his laughter reminding him of his actions,
When Sharma was caught with that awful catch.
Yeah ball was on their CSK court and MI was saddened seeing the chaos.
He briskly asked her to savour the lays and CSK will win and there's nothing new to it.

She had full trust on Bhaji he was now on the pavilion, a dead ball, 1run, possible strikeout and boom.
David and Shane had a minor talk, maybe they planned how to win this off.
Toss was won by us, he again piped;
Do not worry, it will be on that, she chimed.

Overs after over, Mohit Sharma was at strike, Pandya was at the other end,

He winked at Tara, she was ready to blow off,
His knuckles ready to piss and she hauled.
With tongue out teasing to losing the final hope.
She took all the revenge when finally, MI won.

D. Agilan

Agilan, the writer, who came to the world, to express the thoughts of life. He is not a great writer, but a scribbler.

The World Game War

They are fighting for their country's victory,

They use bat and ball only as a weapon to make the country's win,

They sometimes hurt themselves because of the flow on the ground,

They are looking for us medicine for their wound for the country's success,

This is not a game war
But, the cold war between two peoples,
Which is known as "World cup".

Sonnet From A Big Fan

I am your big fan,
Even I didn't know about you.
I am your big fan;
Even I didn't learn about you;
I am your big fan,
Even I didn't speak about you;
I am your big fan,
Even I didn't play with you;
I am your big fan,
Even I didn't cry for you;
I will be always your big fan,
Not because of your name;
But the medicine you are
Giving for our mind and heart.

Nikhitha Vanga

She is pursuing Engineering in the Department of Electronics and communication at Hyderabad. She is known for her creativity and innovation. Writing short stories, poems are her passion. She lives vicariously through Herself all day long

Cricket...! Cricket...! Cricket...!

From a 10year old kid to the late '80s uncle are in love with this unique game called cricket. cricket is like a fancy, fairy Disney World for us and the cricketers are our real superstars. The efforts they put in each match, in each ball is astounding. Sachin's centuries, Dhoni's swag and the latest Virat's aggressive looks. Who else denies from falling in love with them??
While India must be proud for having such extraordinary players who are beautiful inside out.

Eight powerful teams
Eight amazing captains
Each of our favourite player in new jerseys, playing on the other side, yet supporting each other, Isn't this eye feast??
What an amazing idea, this IPL is...! bringing out the new talents each year, breaking the old records, setting the new boundaries. With each year, our excitement gets doubled, our plans get cancelled only to watch IPL and saving money to buy the tickets to watch our favourite team playing, fighting with my mom for the remote to watch IPL is a never-ending cycle though

Jude Fernandes

Graduating with a B.A. in English (Honours) Degree from M.E.S. College - Zuarinagar in 2020, Jude is an enthusiastic student residing in Vasco da Gama, Goa - India. His passionate talents in literature, creative writing, reading, music, singing, acting, sketching and public speaking have secured numerous awards at school, college and State levels. He is also a co-author of 40+ national and international anthologies. Instagram Handle: jude_fernandes_official. Currently working on his solo poetry collection, Jude aspires to be an English professor and an established author in the near future. Life's experiences unleash true potential within him!

From narrow lanes of slums,
to international stadiums:
cricket resonates with glory
in millions of hearts and minds!

Passion, skill and dedication:
they fill ardent lovers with jubilation!
It all begins with a humble bat and ball...
Witness the wild cheers that erupt!

Team coordination is the key
to win mass praise, not just the match...
More than a career or entertainment,
cricket is love, cricket brings joy!

Follow the rules, maintain your focus;
concentrate on what matters the most:
work hard, work steadily...
victory shall be thy reward!

Mansha Poddar

Mansha Poddar was born on 14th August 2003 in Sambalpur, Odisha. Since childhood, her parents and teachers supported her in her writing skills. She is a sprouting bud of fantasy who loves to dress up her words. She aspires to become a well-known writer as well as a Forest Officer. She is a spiritual person and a devotee of God despite of any religion. You can reach her for more of her scribbled writings on Instagram at @perpetual_covet.

Cricket

When India won the toss,
Sachin became the boss.
When Sachin hit a century,
Dravid got an injury.
When Sachin was out,
India was in doubt.
When Shahid Afridi beat a four,
David's injury was a cure.
When Pakistan lost the match,
Sachin became the man of the match.
When Wasim Akram was drinking coffee,
Sachin in both hands got the trophy.

आईपीएल

ये खेल नही एक त्यौहार है,
पूरा भारत करता इसका इंतज़ार है!
माहौल भी बनाते ऐसा की दुनिया मे,
लोग इसके आने का करते इंतज़ार है,
सट्टेबाज भी इसमे खूब कमाते है,
हर गेंद पे अंपायर अपना कमाल दिखाते है,
आठ टीमें भी इसमे टकराती है,
पर हमेशा आर.सी.बी सबका दिल जीत जाती है,
सी .एस.के की टीम भी खतरनाक बन जाती है,
हर टीम में वो अपना खौफ बनाती है,
अस.आर.एच् की टीम ने भी कमाल दिखाया है,
वार्नर के दम पे ईतिहास है,
पंजाब की टीम के क्या कहने जनाब,
गेल के दम अपनी उम्मीद जागती है,
बौलिंग में सबसे ज़्यादा रन वही खाती हैं,
के .के.आर की टीम का भी अलग जलवा है,
रसेल के दम पे बोलता इनका बल्ला है,
दिल्ली की टीम भी बड़ी खयाली है,
रबाडा की गेंदबाजी अच्छे अच्छों पर भारी है,
सुपर ओवर में वो अपना कमाल दिखाता है,
सारे बल्लेबाज़ों के आखो में आंसू लाता है,
तो यही है पूरे आईपीएल की कहानी एक,
छोटी सी जुबानी!

Vishal Agrawal

He was born and brought up in Mathura Uttar Pradesh. He is an engineering student pursuing his bachelor's degree from GLA University Mathura. He is multi-talented and multi-tasker. He likes singing, sketching and writing. he writes to expresses his feeling and emotions on the paper. Sometimes his quotes and Shayari inspire and motivate people. He feels that his hard work is his biggest strength.

He is co-author of 15+ books which also include vajra world record holder anthology. He is the compiler of 3 books: The mysterious life, Verses of life and My Country My pride

ये खेल बड़ा निराला है

ये खेल बड़ा निराला है
सब मुल्को में प्यारा है,

जहाँ विराट, डिविलयर्स की यारी है
ये जोड़ी सबसे प्यारी है,
जहाँ राशिद को फिरकी
माही को हेलीकाप्टर शॉट से प्यार है,
ये खेल बड़ा ही अद्धभुत
भारत का त्यौहार है,

चौको, छक्कों की बौछार यहाँ
रनों की बरसात है,
जहाँ भाईचारा, खेल भावना
विश्व प्रसिद्ध बिख्यात है,

चकाचोंध और हल्ले गुल्ले से
भरा रहता पूरा मैदान,
कभी कोहली कभी धोनी
लोगों के होठों पर जिनका नाम है,
ये खेल बड़ा ही अद्‌भुत
मनोरंजन की पहचान है।

Harshal Raju Ninawe

She is studied in S.N.Mor College, Tumsar
She loves reading books, cooking and writing poems

वो रोमांच आखरी कुछ पल का,
हर एक गेंद , कर दे बेकल सा |
चौके - छक्के पर तालिया
विकेट गिरने पर गालीया,
बढते खेल संग जैसे रुकता जाए दम
कुछ ऐसे है यार क्रिकेट और हम ||

टी.वी देख इतनी दूर से सलाह दें
ना मानने पर गालिया भी अथाह दें |
ना पास हो गेंद ना ही बल्ला,
पर हर आती गेंदपर मचाये हल्ला |
बदलते खेल संग हात - पांव चल रहे हैं
जैसे खेल वो खिलाडी नहीं, हम ही खैल रहे हैं |

गिनती रखते हर एक रन की
गतिविधीयां बढ जाए, सोच - विचांरते मन की |
जिते तो जैसे कोई त्योहारहो,
हारने पर जैसे जाते बिमार हो,
हो हारने की कगार पर तो क्या,
जीत की उम्मीद रखें आखरी गेंद तक हरदम,
कुछ ऐसे है यार क्रिकेट और हम ||

विनय झा

नाम - विनय झा ।
पता-ग्राम-मेंहथ जिला - मधुबनी बिहार

हम लगातार फ्रीलेंसर के रूप में अलग-अलग सोशल मीडिया प्लेटफॉर्म और वेबपोर्टल के लिए कहानी, कविता, आर्टीकल, और समसामयिक विषय पर लगातार लिखते रहे है।अलग -अलग विषय जैसे राजनीति, खेल और सिनेमा पर निरन्तर हमारा लेख आता रहा है

क्रिकेट का सफर

भारतीयों के दिल में क्रिकेट की दीवानगी का आलम यह है कि, यहाँ हर खाली जगह को क्रिकेट के मैदान की तरह देखा जाता है।और यहाँ लोग क्रिकेट को धर्म तो सचिन तेंदुलकर को उसका भगवान के रूप में देखते है।

आज जब पूरी दुनिया कोरोना महामारी से परेशान और हताश है ।उस वक़्त आईपीएल का शुरू होना मानो पतझड़ के बाद बसंत के आगमन जैसा एहसास दे रहा है।

15 मार्च 1877 में पहले अंतरराष्ट्रीय टेस्ट क्रिकेट मैच हो, या फिर 5 जनवरी 1971 को पहला एक दिवसीय मैच से टी ट्वेंटी तक का सफर ।बदलते वक़्त के साथ क्रिकेट ने अपने प्रारूप को लगातार बदलता रहा यही कारण है कि इस खेल का रोमांच समय के साथ और निखरता गया।

21वी सदी के शुरुआत से ही दुनिया बड़ी तेजी से बदलने लगी ।ऐसे में क्रिकेट ने एक बार फिर अपने प्रारूप को बदला जिसे हम टी ट्वेंटी के नाम से जानते है

साल 2003 में यूनाइटेड किंगडम में पहली बार बीस ओवर का मैच खेला गया । ठीक चार साल बाद 2007 में पहला टी ट्वेंटी वर्ल्डकप का आयोजन हुआ ।लंबे बाल वाला एक देहाती खिलाड़ी के नेतृत्व में भारत पहला टी ट्वेंटी वर्ल्डकप जीतकर पूरे दुनिया में क्रिकेट के इस फॉर्मेट में अपना बादशाहत कायम कर लिया । उस लंबे बाल वाले खिलाड़ी को हम कैप्टन कूल धोनी के नाम से जानते है।

टी ट्वेंटी क्रिकेट की बढ़ती हुई लोकप्रियता को देखते हुए साल 2008 में बीसीसीआई ने ललित मोदी के देख-रेख में इडियन प्रीमियर लीग (आईपीएल) की शुरुआत की जो कि दुनिया के बाकि लीग से

बिल्कुल अलग था। जो विशुद्ध रूप से एक बिजनेस मॉडल की तरह है । इसमें कुल आठ टीमों को शामिल किया गया सबके अलग-अलग फ्रंचाईजी जो उस टीम का मालिक भी है।

पहले आईपीएल में सबको चौकाते हुए राजस्थान रॉयल ने चेन्नई सुपर किंग को हराकर पहला टाइटल अपने नाम किया । तबसे लेकर आजतक जहाँ मुंबई इंडियन ने सबसे अधिक बार आईपीएल फाइनल जीता ,वही चैन्नई सुपर किंग सबसे अधिक बार फाइनल खेलने का रिकॉर्ड अपने नाम किया है। सबसे अधिक रन बनाने के मामले में विराट कोहली सबसे ऊपर है तो सर्वाधिक विकेट लेने का रिकॉर्ड लासिथ मलिंगा के नाम है ।

आईपीएल के रूप में भारत ने एक ऐसे लीग का शुरुआत किया जो कि बॉलीबुड की फ़िल्म की तरह है जिसमे तीन घंटे के दौरान आपको ग्लैमर, मस्ती, चकाचौंध रोमांच ,उत्साह और सस्पेंस हर चीज देखने को मिलता है पूरा पैसा वसूल ।

Tushar Bhakte

Professionally Tushar is a mechanical engineer. As engineers satisfy both themselves & humanity, which is the reason for his
passion for engineering. He is a full-time worker in the corporate world
but has a busy head that always bombards with thoughts, ideas and
recalls to things which he has read or learned. It's like having boiling water in a pressure cooker. Writing will be like opening the
valve and releasing the steam (ideas). You can follow his blog named "Ethereal Love".

The Frenzy IPL season in the bleak of the pandemic

IPL has always been an electrifying experience may it be for the viewers or the big franchises. The reason being cricket which once upon a time was treated as a sport, now it means much more - emotion, for some religion too.
This year even though the matches are played with vacant seats, however, they aren't vacant with any less emotion than that of earlier seasons. Everyday 7.30 p.m. the TV sets are on, and people filled with all the emotion and enthusiasm are waiting for a thrilling contest. What can you expect more from us; cricket lovers.

We are in blue, we are in yellow, we are in red, we are in pink and we will be there if not physically then virtually, and there will be a voice echoing - "Dhoni, Dhoni" or "Virat Virat" - and we will wait till the last ball to be hit as a six.
We will wait to see the perfect yorkers, the huge sixes and nevertheless we will witness the new records.

There lies a hope ahead, just like in a cricket match for us to overcome - the pandemic - to see the world again. For travellers to roam the world, for children to go to schools and at last the humongous cricket stadiums to be filled again with us!!!

Samiksha Wasudeo Kumbhare

She completed her graduation in B.Voc (software development) at J.M. Patel college, Bhandara.

त्याला क्रिकेट ऐसे नाव आहे

तसं पाहायला गेलो तर फक्त एक खेळच आहे
पण खेळताना जणू, युद्धाचा आव आहे,
त्याला क्रिकेट ऐसे नाव आहे

जी सरता सरत नाही, कधी संपत नाही
अशी ज्यात फक्त जिंकण्याची हाव आहे
त्याला क्रिकेट ऐसे नाव आहे

ही आहे संधी, दाखवून द्या जगास
की कोण चोर अन कोण साव आहे
त्याला क्रिकेट ऐसे नाव आहे

लक्ष्य आहे जिंकण्याचे, जिंकायचेच
खेळ फक्त नाही, आयुष्याचा डाव आहे
त्याला क्रिकेट ऐसे नाव आहे!!

Sarabjot Purba

Sarabjot Purba lives in Kotkapura, Punjab. He wrote a poem for the first time when he was in class XI. After this While studying E.T.T., he started writing poems as well as essays and stories. He has given the thoughts of his mind in the form of a book. Whose name is 'Kuz Vichar'. He also wrote some pages related to E.T.T. College time. He has written something on every subject. He often writes on issues of society. He mostly uses Punjabi language.

Insta id - @Purba_poetry

क्रिकेट के दीवाने है हम,
बचपन से ही तो खेलते है।
अब जब काम कुछ बढ़ गए है,
आई.पी.एल ही बस देखते है।
बचपन याद आ जाता है,
जब बल्लेबाजी धोनी करता है।
गेंद भी धीमी हो जाती है,
हर गेंदबाज उनसे डरता है।
मन करता है वहाँ जाकर देखूँ,
टी. वी. तो देखा कई बार है।
चोके-छक्के लगने के बाद,
नाचने का इंतजार है।
बच्चों में इसका जोश बहुत है,
हर कोई खेलना चाहता है।
बुढ़े भी कुछ देखते है,
मन उनका भी बहलाता है।

Khushbu Rathore

An independent soul who likes to read, write, pants and design. A girl who, through poetry, expresses her feelings and enjoys comfort.
B. Ed is very talented girl with getting education. A proud girl from Pali district of Rajasthan receives her education during the day and most of her time in the night gives her time to the writing work. She is Khusbu Rathore and is delighted to be a part of this anthology
Instagram =@khushburathore1913

आईपीएल का बोलबाला

कभी एक आईपीएल ऐसा भी हो
जिसका खुमार आईपीएल जैसा हो

कभी ऐसी गुगली आए
कि बेरोजगार आउट हो जाए
गरीबी पगबाधा हो
मंहगाई रन आउट हो
भ्रष्टाचार जो लगातार स्कोर कार्ड बढ़ाए जा रहा है
उनका इनसे भी बुरा हाल हो जाए
जब एक लंबी हिट लगाए तो
बाउण्ड्री लाइन पर कैच आउट हो जाए
हमेशा मैच हमारा भारत ही जीते
ग्राउंड चाहे जैसा भी हो

कभी एक आईपीएल ऐसा भी हो
जिसका खुमार आईपीएल जैसा हो

हम सभी हिन्दुस्तानी एक टीम है
हमारा एकता अखंडता में ना कहीं फिक्सिंग हो
दंगों की ना डेड बॉल हो
भेदभाव की ना नोबॉल हो
लिंगभेद करने वालों पर सदा प्रतिबंध लगे
परस्पर प्यार और भाईचारा का मैच हो

Spoorthi H C

Spoorthi H C is a writer from Chikkamagaluru, Karnataka with over 20+ anthologies published as a co-author. She began writing while still a student and aspires to be a full-time writer someday. She is a classical singer and dancer.

She also writes in Kannada and has her work published in various newspapers and magazines from time to time. She also publishes her Kannada poetry on Instagram @kavithegala_saalu. An optimistic individual with an infectious smile, she believes that words provide the best comfort at all times.

IPL = Happiness

We all know that 2020 is one of the pandemic years where everyone is fenced in the home. But at this time IPL (Indian Premier League) is one big festivity that occurred. Finally, after long discussions and squabble cricket committee decided to start this season with the same enthusiasm and accomplishment. Whatever it maybe we are all started to gaze at our favourite teams by screaming, looking at their competition also our favourite captain, players etc..., As usual, the craze for RCB team is never-ending. Also, the crazy battle between RCB and CSK fans is just terrific. Whatever the team is but the game will be more fetching till the last ball. That commentary from the senior players is just impressive, those boundaries, sixes out of the stadium, quick stumpings, wickets are incredible and grand. Indian Premier League is one the best platform for every young cricketer to showcase their talent also it's a good opportunity for cricket board to see the tactics of the players.

Jeevitha.S

She is a girl with stupendous writing skills. Her heart is a castle abound with unbreakable courage, being contained with enticing dreams. Penning is her way of spreading aesthetic vibes among her readers. Being a libertarian is her pride. She loves to be a unicorn amidst the flock of sheep's!

Dearest Captain Cool!

To the legend who made me watch cricket as if I'm a deadliest fan of it. I'm not such a fan of cricket, but I'm a versatile fan of you. I don't watch cricket to admire your helicopter shots, but I watch it to see you smile and your smile just melts my heart out! A smile with satisfaction from the coolest captain ever, who won't get mesmerized even after seeing that. Not as a cricketer alone but you have captured a prominent place in our hearts as a good human being with a best soul. An eminent hard worker you are in whatever you do, always wondering how a man could be so cool in all circumstances, it's because he knows all the pros and cons of life. Thank you for being the hope of cricket and no one can replace MSD in the legacy of cricket. Our love towards you never ends Captain Cool, from one of your fans among millions with endless love!

Auqib Hassan

Auqib hassan is a soulful writer who emanates from Budgam (Kashmir). And is presently a student of cluster university where he's pursuing his bachelor's degree. His writings don't have fixed boundaries to communicate, he writes everything that he feels around and within. The uniqueness of his write-ups is that he can express notions lucidly and brevity. He's sure that one day he'll scintillate like Sirius and people will endeavour to adapt the light of his fascinating and deep words.

Instagram ID: @dr_transplant_soul

Cricket Is Not Just A Sport But An Ultimate Victory Of Sportsmen's

I will not mention that cricket is only a game, rather it's a great achievement that everyone can't achieve without proper utilisation, courage, confidence and determination.

We all have given it a try in Gullies and little fields for Timepass and fun, but very few people get this in veins and nerves that in which they can see their future. Initially, they treat it as passion and with time this hard work, dedication and passion turns into strong enthusiasm which makes them keen and highly developed towards their goal and then they call it an ambition for which they have diligently devoted their zest.

We have the history of great cricketers from end parts of the world, who have made cricket their profession and pride for their Nations. I would like to mention Imran Khan,

M.S Dhoni, Shahid Afridi and Sachin Tendulkar who have always been strong like steel and concrete for their Team and the reputation of Nation.

There's an evolution change in the field of cricket. This time we have 3 types of format cricket played at the international level – Test matches, One-Day Internationals and Twenty20 Internationals. These matches are played under the rules and regulations approved by the International Cricket Council, which also provides match officials for them.

Why cricket is so popular?

Before we start answering the big question, it might be interesting to know how popular cricket really is worldwide. Well, the short answer is it's the world's second most popular sport, right after soccer.

And if we see the regional Popularity throughout the World then India ranks the first with 100 popularity and then Pakistan with 70 popularity and so on...

"Believe it or not, the sport of Cricket was once one of the more popular sports in the United States. Today, cricket is most popular in England, India and Australia. But over the last few decades increasing numbers of Indians and West Indians have moved to the United States, naturally increasing the sport's popularity. Last April, ESPN broadcasted an Indian Premier League cricket match between India and Sri Lanka, and matches like these are now regularly streamed online and through digital media. ESPN estimates that the growing cricket market in the United States currently consists of about 30 million fans, with New York City being one of the biggest hotbeds for the sport."

"Every athlete is an inspiration and every game needs a valiant comrade with the fact that 'it all starts with a Trivial".

Debangsh Das

Debangsh Das was born on 21-06-1999 to Kanak Das in Patna. He is an Engineering student who loves to innovate new things. His hobbies are writing shayaris, poems, singing, and reading. His writings are spilled out from the pen of his pain and from his own experiences.

IPL

Yu to India mai na jane kitne teyohar hote hai...
Aur har teyohar hum India vale bade shan se manate hai...
Par IPL hi ek esa teyohar hai jisse manane...
Bahar se bhi log taiyaar ho chale aate hai...

Cricket

Jaha shor hai ...
Vha kuch to hai...
Jha josh hai...
Vha koi to hai ...
Jisse hosh nhi...
Usmai kuch to hai...
Ussi tarah ye cricket sirf ek game nhi...
Game se bhi badhkar kuch to hai...

IPL

Insan to insan ko hi pyar krta hai...
Dil to Dil pe hi marta hai...
Yu to pure saal yha har koi...
khud mai hi madhosh rehta hai...
Par phir sab ek hote hai...
jab vo khel Ka badshaah...
IPL Chala aata hai...

Sumedha Dutt

Sumedha Dutt is a Journalism and Mass Communication graduate, who believes in the power of positive thinking. She writes what she believes, experience and feels. Her pieces of poetry have a special connection with her life. "Magic can happen anytime, any day”, "love can be recreated" she believes.

She is pursuing Event Management as a career and Writing as a passion.

क्रिकेट की यादें

बचपन के वो दिन,
आज भी याद है मुझे
घर के इकलौते टी.वी के सामने,
भीड़ जो लगा करती थी
चाचा की ढोलक छक्के पर जब,
ज़ोर से बजा करती थी
मैच देखने वालो का शोर जब,
मोहल्ले में गूंजा करता था
घर का बच्चा बच्चा जब,
सचिन, गांगुली को फॉलो करता था

वर्ल्ड कप के हर मैच का,
बेसब्री से इंतज़ार करते थे
नीली जर्सी पहन के,
इंडिया का गुणगान करते थे
मां उधर मंदिर में,
दिया जलाना कभी ना भूलती थी
मैच के प्रारंभ में नारियल,
टी.वी के सामने फोड़ती थी
हर घर की कुछ ऐसी ही,
कहानी हुआ करती थी

आईपीएल जो आता था,
क्रिकेट टीम ज़रूर बटती थी
जो कभी साथ खेलते थे,
उन्हीं में जंग छिड़ीती थी
नीले रंग की जगह अब,
लाल, पीले और नारंगी ने ले ली थी
फिर भी सब साथ,

मिलकर रहते थे
क्योंकि भारतीय संस्कार की,
बात ही कुछ ऐसी थी

Debanjana Ghatak

Debanjana is a simple girl and down to earth by nature. By profession, she is an English Faculty at a reputed Educational Institution. She is an ardent lover of Nature, animals, Literature and a believer of God. She loves to dream and enjoy dwelling in her fairy-tale land. She loves to enjoy the tiny rays of happiness hidden in the smallest moments of life. In short, she describes herself as a dreamer and believer. Whenever she felt the presence and beauty of love and got a smell of Nature, new poetry or a story took birth. She believes in the philosophy of never giving up. She doesn't give up dreaming and believing in what she believes. My Instagram id: @dgwrites_

My Best Cricketer and Motivator

Dear Sourav,

You are my inspiration and motivator. I came to know about you from my grandfather and elder cousin brothers who are cricket fanatics and your fans as well. It was 1997 when I first saw your match on TV as a little kid and started growing passion for the game. Slowly I became your fan and my love for cricket grew like never before. I was a sport-loving person from my childhood days but never was a mad supporter of any game as I became for cricket and for you.

At school, I opted for Games as a subject because I wanted to play cricket with my friends and they were mostly boys because girls took Economics and Accountancy as they didn't want to bask in the sun and run in the sports ground. I even wished to become a cricketer and dreamt to play in the International Women's Cricket team but alas, my parents didn't allow me to do it. Yes, I gave up my dream but never stopped loving and respecting you, dear brother. I call you 'dada' since I saw you first time on TV and wished if I had a brother like you.

Now I have grown up and have other priorities but my love for cricket is still alive in my heart. Now you are the President of BCCI and this makes me so proud. I was, I am and will always be your fan no matter how perfect other players are but for me, you are the best cricketer and I will always be your supporter.

From,

Your loving sister

Sahaj Sabharwal

PERSONALITY OF JAMMU, INDIA

He loves writing poems and thoughts. He lives in Jammu city, Jammu and Kashmir, India. His date of birth is 17th March, 2002. He has been awarded many awards in poem writing at State level, National and international level. He was also selected to be invited for the INTERNATIONAL WRITERS MEETING IN TARIJA and HUNGARY, EUROPE. He was awarded with the INTERNATIONAL DIPLOMA IN WRITING and INTERNATIONAL MERIT CERTIFICATE IN WRITING and was PUBLISHED by THE YOUNG WRITERS ASSOCIATION IN UK.

महेन्द्र सिंह धोनी

क्रिकेट तो एक ज़रिया था,
देश के लिए इनके दिल में कुछ कर दिखाने का बहता दरिया था।

ये अपने जीवन की समस्याओं से न डरे,
अच्छे से लड़े, तब कहीं जाकर आगे बढ़े।

जितनी देर ये खेले, इन्होंने आराम से अच्छा समय बिताया,
सन् 2011 में इनकी कप्तानी ने भारत को विश्व कप जितिया।

बल्लेबाजी, गेंदबाजी, विकेट कीपिंग आधि सबमें अच्छे थे,
यही नहीं, ये मन के साफ और दिल के बहुत अच्छे थे।

कैप्टन बनकर खिलाड़ियों को अच्छे से खेलना सिखाया,
भारत देश किसी से कम नहीं है, पूरे विश्व को दिखाया।

Players are those who dare to care,
Not just in bulk but in rare.

Shivika Sharma

Shivika Sharma is a writer.
She is a college student. She lives in Kawardha Chhattisgarh. She loves to write poems, quotes & shayaris etc. She used yourquote app for presenting her views. Her insta handle is @shivika1108

क्रिकेट

खेल-खेल में लोग यहां,
इस संसार को जीत लेते है।
बेसब्री से लोग यहां,
क्रिकेट का इंतजार करते हैं।।

क्रिकेट एक ऐसा खेल,
जो लोगों को बेहद ही पसंद हैं।
इसे देखने को तो,
लोगों में बेहद ही उमंग हैं।।

हर बार जीत हो इंडिया की,
लोगों की यही ख्वाहिश रहती हैं।
और लोग तो इसे देखने को,
सदैव आगे रहते हैं।।

एक सप्ताह पहले से ही,
इसे देखने की तैयारी में लोग लग जाते हैं।
और जब ये टी.वी पर आने लगे,
तो फिर लोगों को कुछ नज़र नहीं आते हैं।।

बहुत पसंद हैं हर किसी को,
बेट-बॉल का यह खेल।
बचपन से ही लोग इसे,
खेलने में लग जाते हैं।।

नाम कमाया है बड़े-बड़े लोगों ने,
इस खेल को खेलकर।
यह खेल तो दुनिया में,
अंतरराष्ट्रीय में खेला जाता हैं।।

विराट कोहली,सचिन तेंदुलकर जैसे खिलाड़ी,
इस खेल से आगे बढ़े हैं।
महेंद्र सिंह धोनी भी इस खेल से ही,
अपना नाम बनाए हैं।।

क्रिकेट के नाम से ही लोगों में,
बेहद उमंग भर आती हैं।
और इसे देखने को तो,
लोगों में जोश ही जग जाती हैं।।

पसंद हैं मुझे भी यह खेल,
मैं भी बचपन में खेला करती थी।
अभी भी शौक जब लगता है,
तो अब भी मैं खेल लिया करती हूं।

Priya Jha

Priya Jha is a writer from Madhubani, Bihar. She is doing her masters from IMS Noida. She has started writing from mid of 2018. And till now there are lots of poems, which she has written.

Most of her written poems are based on truth.

She loves to write on social issue, and and mostly on love.

Insta ID - @Crystal_priya

Cricket Again

Cricket is just not a game to play,
It's not only a word to say,
The ball from which the cricketers play is not a toy,
It's a feeling, an emotion, and all that sweet bond which filled our family with joy,

Take out your cricket bat, it's time to play again,
All the memories which had been vanished by the time,
All we need is to build that once again,
The umpire, the batsman, the ballers, and the ball,
All are waiting to scream with happiness by all their heart and soul.

Khushi Mohan Kothale

Khushi aka MC_RUDE is a student of biotechnology from Nagpur, Maharashtra. Her passion for writing is never defined. Moreover, she's also a rapper and lyricist.
Instagram ID - @__mc_rude__

Am I only the one?

Am I only the one,
Who breathes every over?
Am I only the one,
Who feels ever runner?
Am I only the one,
Who cries when team loses?
Am I only the one,
Who sits Infront of TV wearing a Jersey and cheering out loud?
Am I only the one,
Who bets with dad?
Am I only the one,
Who bursts out on shots?
Am I only the one,
Who screams MSD for helicopter?
Am I only the one,
Who falls for Virat's aggression?
Am I only the one,
Who smiles at Rohit?
Am I only the one,
Who waits for Rayudu?
Am I only the one,
Who misses Raina?
Am I only the one,
Who reads ABD and misses the 'C'?
Am I only the one,
Who sets the barrier free?
Am I only the one,
Who sigh when it's lbw?
Am I only the one,
Who cry for Warner?

Am I only the one,

Who grins at Chawla?
An I only the one,
Who admires Jadeja?
Am I only the one,
Who's carefree for Shaw?
Am I only the one,
Who stay awake for Russel?
Am I only the one,
Who announces Champion for Gayle?
Am I only the one,
Who sings Lil Wayne?
Am I only the one,
Whose blood is filled with IPL and heart beats team India?

Sahina Ghugha

Sahina Ghugha from Jamnagar city of Gujarat is student of B.com at Saurashtra university, Rajkot. She is state level champion in poetry contest 2017. She wants to be amazing Writer.

Instagram ID:- @itz_sahina_write

इंडिया का त्यौहार

कुछ अलग मज़ा है इसका
कुछ अलग ही है अंदाज़।
अहेसास बेमतलब खुशियों का
ऐसा ये क्रिकेट है मेरे यार।

कुछ खास लगता इन दिनों
भारत का हर नौजवान।
राष्ट्रीय खेल हॉकी सही
क्रिकेट तो रहेगा हमारी जान।

इंडियन प्रीमियर लीग सुनते ही
चढ़ जाता अलग खुशियों का खुमार।
खड़ा हो जाए वो शख्स भी देखने
जिसको चढ़ा हुआ हो बुखार।

भूलकर मूवी, भूल जाए हर चैनल
सब बैठ जाते है देखने क्रिकेट।
खाना पानी कुछ याद ना आए
ऐसा ही है इंडिया का त्यौहार।

Surekha Wankhede

Surekha Wankhede, a very passionate girl. She belongs to city of Oranges, Nagpur, Maharashtra. Apart than writing she loves to do Classical dance, glass painting. She has worked as co-author in many anthologies including World Records too. An optimistic and keen observant girl.

Cricket Is Love

Even stranger became my friend when he/she speaking about Cricket.
Cricket is the only thing which makes us forget the bad time for a while.
Cricket is love.

Piyush Bhardwaj

Piyush is a writer who lives in Faridabad (Haryana). He studies in class 11. He has won many e-certificates in online writing competitions. He is in the early part of the writing journey. Everyone has something unique about them. It's just about putting it on a paper in a fun and easy-to-read way.

क्रिकेट का त्योहार - आईपीएल

फिर आया क्रिकेट का त्यौहार है
अब सब पे चढ़ा क्रिकेट का बुखार है
आईपीएल का जज्बा इतना जोरदार है
चाहे बच्चा हो या बुजुर्ग होता सबको सिर्फ मैच का इंतेज़ार है
सिक्का उछालकर मैच को शुरू किया जाता है
कौन बैटिंग करेगा या बॉलिंग ये तय किया जाता है
फिर रोमांच का सिलसिला चालू होता है
पूरे परिवार के साथ बैठकर मैच देखा जाता है
होता एक है पूरा परिवार मगर सपोर्ट अलग अलग टीम को किया जाता है
आखिर यही तो है आईपीएल की बात
टीम अलग अलग हो फिर भी पूरा इंडिया एक हो जाता है

टी-20 क्रिकेट

टी-20 क्रिकेट तो सबकी जान है
हर इंसान के दिल मे इसका अलग ही स्थान है
बैट बॉल और स्टंप्स का है ये अद्‌भुत खेल
कभी लगे चोका,छक्का तो कभी बॉल और स्टम्प्स का मेल
शुरू के 6 ओवर्स में रहते है 2 खिलाड़ी 30 गज के दायरे के बाहर
और होती है बाउंड्रीज की बौछार
टी-20 फॉरमेट की तो बात ही अलग है
इसे देखने की हर किसी में अलग ही तलब है

Karan Vijay Nandanwar

Karan Nandanwar was born in the Mohadi, Dist.~Bhandara. He is Diploma 3rd Year pursuing. Thriller and Suspense is her favourite genre. He loves travelling, photoshoot, mobile shoot and listening to music.
Instagram ID - @naturelover; @nirajnandanwar

चेन्नई सुपर किंग्सचा चाहता

एक बाजी हार गया तो क्या अभी भी करोडो दिलों पर
आज भी राज चलता हैं हमारा!!

माही साठी प्रेम

हर कोई चाहता हैं सी. एस.के. को पर तू चाहती हैं मै MI को प्यार करू,
तेरा तो पता नहीं पर ये दिल भी राजी
नहीं होंगा ये दिल तो सिर्फ सी. एस.के. के लिए हैं।

Aastha Shukla

Aastha Shukla (beh_lfz) is a medical student and a new writer of 17 years. She started her writing by getting encouragement from her father. She is a writer on Instagram also with name @beh_lfz. She is also a motivational speaker. In a very young age, she helps most of the people to get off from their situation and with her writing, she inspires many people. She wants to aware the people from her writing. From a very small place, she has higher dreams.

आईपीएल का आगमन

इस कोविड 19 की टेंशन के समय,
कुछ तो अच्छा हुआ है ।
आईपीएल ने आके सबको खुश किया है ।
पूरे दिन का इंतज़ार होता है,
फिर 7.30 बजे आईपीएल का जब आगमं होता है।
नज़रे टी वी से चिपक जाती है,
बच्चा हो या बड़ा,
लड़किया भी आईपीएल का मोज उठती है
चलो कुछ तो राहत मिली है इस महामारी से,
सब हो ही चुका है इस साल,
अब छक्के चोक्को की बारी है ।

मैदान मे माही

सबके लिए कुछ और नाम होगा सुकूँ का,
हम तो माही को मैदान मे देख के सुकूँ पा रहे है,
हम आईपीएल फैंस है यारों,
अब दिल को आईपीएल से बहला रहे हैं ।
मैदान मे जब वो आता है,
शोर से पूरा स्टेडियम नाच जाता है ।
उसके आगे गिडर ही नहीं,
शेर तक काँप जाता है ।
चीनाइ सुपर किंग्स की शान है वो,
इंडिया के हर प्लेयर की जान है वो ।
हर चेहरा खुशी से खिल जाता है,
जब धोनी मैदान मे आता है ।

Ishwari Kishor Shirur

मी ईश्वरी किशोर शिरुर. अंबरनाथ येथे राहत असून रुईया महाविद्यालयात तृतीय वर्ष कला शाखेत शिकत आहे. परीघावरच्या कविता, अस्मिता आणि सुगंध सोबतीचा या काव्यसंग्रहात स्वलिखित कविता प्रकाशित झाल्या असून स्टोरी मिरर मध्ये माझ्या स्वलिखित कथेला Best Author Of The Week प्रमाणपत्र देऊन सन्मानित केले आहे.

मी अनुभवलेला क्रिकेट...!

क्रिकेट हा शब्द नुसता ऐकला जरी तरी एक वेगळीच उमाळी फुलून येते. तस बघायला गेलं तर क्रिकेट हा मुलांचा प्रचंड आवडता खेळ. पण एक मुलगी म्हणून क्रिकेट कडे बघण्याचा माझा दृष्टिकोन जरा वेगळाच आहे. हा आता, हातात बॅट धरण्याची वेळ कधी माझ्यावर आली नसली तरी वर्ल्ड कप ची मॅच बघण्यात मला अजूनही मजा येते. प्रत्येक बालमन तर आपल्या कुमार वयात सचिन तेंडुलकर होण्याचं स्वप्न अंतरमनात रंगवत असतचं. क्रिकेट सोबत प्रत्येकाच्या काही ना काही आठवणी जोडलेल्या असतात. माझीही अशीच एक आठवण क्रिकेटशी जोडलेली आहे. ही क्रिकेट ची आठवण म्हणजे २०११ची भारत विरुद्ध श्रीलंका वर्ल्ड कप मॅच. मला तर वाटतयं की, हि मॅच कोणीच विसरू शकणार नाही. तशीच काहीशी ही मॅच रंगली होती. हा चुरशीचा सामना चालू असताना माझ्या घरातलं वातावरण फारच लक्षवेधी स्वरुपाचं होतं.

घरात बऱ्यापैकी मोठा टिव्ही असल्यामुळे आजूबाजूची चिल्ली पिल्ली कारटी आमच्या घरी येऊन बसली होती. मॅच चालू होण्या आधीच घरात सचिन च्या नावाचा जयघोष चालू होता. बाहेरील वातावरण देखील क्रिकेटमय झाले होतेे. मॅच चालू झाल्यावर टिव्ही समोर बसलेली आमची चिल्लर पार्टी हातात पॉपकॉर्न घेऊन घरात स्टेडियम वाला फिल घेऊन बसली होती. बाबांची त्यांच्या जिवश्य कंठश्य मित्रांसोबत आॅनलाइन बेटिंग चालू होती. शिवाय बाबांना पुर्णपणे खात्री असल्यामुळे मोठ्या मनाने इंडियाच्या बाजूने बेटिंग लावली होती. घरात सर्वात लहान व्यक्तिमत्त्व म्हणजे आमचे उत्साही आजोबा. आजोबा तर थाळी आणि चमचा वाजवत चौकार आणि षटकारांना प्रतिसाद देत होते. देवभोळी आजी देखील अध्यात्म बाजूला ठेवून नातवंडांसोबत सचिन.... सचिन.... असा जयघोष करीत होती. विशेष म्हणजे सासू सुनेच्या मालिका पाहणारी माझी आई देखील स्वयंपाक गृहातून डोकाऊन अधून मधून स्कोर किती झाला? असे विचारत होती. दहावीच्या परिक्षेला बसलेला बिचारा दादा आपल्या छोट्या बहिणीला कधी चॉकलेट कधी आणखी काही अशी

आमीश देऊन बहिणीकडून फ्री कॉमेंट्री काढून घेत होता. लहान बहीण देखील तेवढीच हुशार होती. आपल्याला जे जे पाहिजे त्या सगळ्याची भली मोठी लिस्ट तिने आधीपासूनच तयार ठेवली होती.
महेंद्रसिंह धोनी या मॅच ची कॅप्टनशिप निभावत होता. घरातला सगळा भारताच्या दृष्टिकोनातून ही फारच महत्ताची मॅच होती. कारण या सामन्याअंती भारताला दुसऱ्या वर्ल्ड कपची ट्रॉफी मिळणार होती. सामना खूपच रंगत चालला होता. जशी चौकार आणि षटकारांची उजळणी होत होती अगदी त्याचप्रमाणे विरुद्ध संघाकडून गोलंदाजी देखील तितक्याच आक्रमकतेने होत होती. कधी इंडियाचे पारडे जड तर कधी श्रीलंकेचे पारडे जड. शेवटी तर भारत हा सामना हरणार की काय अशी काहीशी दृश्य डोळे टिपू लागले होते. डोळ्याचे पारणे क्षणभर विश्रांती घ्यायलाही तयार नव्हते. बोर्डाचा अभ्यास करण्याऱ्या दादाला त्याच्या बहिणीने जेव्हा ही परिस्थिती सांगितली तसा दादा बोर्डाचा अभ्यास अक्षरशः बाजूला टाकून बाहेर येऊन टिव्ही समोर बसला. बाबांना तर जवळपास आज माझ्या हाती काही येणार नाही; आज मी बेटिंग हरणार अशा खात्रीत ते तोंडात बोट खालून बसले होते. चिल्लर पार्टी तर पॉपकॉर्न हातात घेऊन नुसतेच तोंड आऽऽ करुन मॅच पाहत होते. उत्साही आजोबांचा उत्साह तर पुर्णतः ठासळून गेला होता. राम कृष्ण हरी, राम कृष्ण हरी म्हणत आजोबा आपल्या खोलीत आराम खुर्चीत जाऊन रेडीओ लावून बसले. आजीने तर जपमाळ हातात घेऊन हरिनाम घेण्याऐवजी इंडियाऽऽऽ इंडियाऽऽ असा जप करुन देवाला साकडे घालू लागली. स्वयंपाक गृहातून डोकावणारी आई स्वतःशीच पुटपुटत होती. 'काय त्या किरकेटचं आकर्षण म्हणून नाय. चांगली मालिका चालू होती; एव्हाना तर सुरेखाच्या सासूने तिला धक्का मारुन घराबाहेर काढले असेल. जाधव काकींची कारटी इथेच मॅच बघायला आली तेवढं एक बरं म्हणायचं. आता उद्या जाधव काकींना विचारायला लागेल. सुरेखाचं काय झालं ते? असे काहीसे आईचे पुटपुटणे नॉनस्टॉप चालूच होते.
हे सारे क्षण कॅमेरा किंवा मोबाईल कॅप्चर करु शकला नसता. म्हणूनच मी हे क्षण माझ्या डोळ्यासकट मनामध्ये आजही टिपून ठेवले आहेत. पण या सामन्याने देखील आमच्या सारख्या चाहत्या वर्गाचा

मान राखला आणि भारताला दुसरा वर्ल्ड कप मिळवून दिला. माझी लहानपणाची खूप छान आठवण आहे ही; जी मी आता ही एखादी मॅच चालू असेल तरी आठवून खदखदून हसते.

Hema Kirthiga J

She is Hema Kirthiga J, and her pen name is sparkle. She is professionally a psychologist and passionately a writer. She heals others but writing heals her. She is a writer, reader, orator and a believer. She is from Chennai. She lives by the principle of inspiring and be inspired. She writes her heart and soul and she deeply believes that the depth of her heart and the nib of her pen are soulfully connected. Writing is an art and she is a proud artist. She loves what she does and loves what she writes. You can reach her at Instagram- @the_pen_queen

Email- inker.sparkle@gmail.com
YourQuote – JKM

What you did to me!!

Eyes on the screen!
Popcorn in the mouth!
Eyes wide!
Hands clutched!
Heart beating fast!
Mind praying god!
Oh my dear!
What you did to me!
You made me to concentrate!
You made me attentive!
You made me crazy!
Just for the last ball of 6!

Sarvesh Bagde

This is Sarvesh Bagde, Hailing from "The City of Oranges" Nagpur, Maharashtra. He is a student of life sciences presently pursuing B.sc Biotechnology from Shri Shivaji Science College, Nagpur.
Writing is his passion and he is penning from last 5 years.
He loves writing Quotes, articles, some short stories etc.
That's not giving you a lot of detail, is it?
Follow him at Blogs-https://sarveshbagde.blogspot.com/?m=1
Instagram - @sarv__eshh
Facebook - Sarvesh Bagde
YourQuote-https://www.yourquote.in/sarveshbagde

IPL Ki Kahani

"CRICKET" ye naam sunte hi pata nhi kyu, sharir me ek alag tarah ka ulhas aur utsah bhar jata hai !
Aur baat agar IPL ki ho to haaye ! Uss urja ki koi seema hi nhi rehti.
Hamare desh me har ek vyakti cricket ko utne hi acche tarike se jaanta hai, jitna ki koi professional player.

Maana ki iss baar corona ke keher k wajah se intazar zara zyada hi lamba chala par sach batau, hamara utsah ek tinka bhi kaam na hua.
Hum to jaise "Aag lage basti me, aur hum apni masti me". Chahe jag me jo ho Jaye, IPL ka fan base Kabhi Kam nhi Hoga.

Hamare liye IPL koi khel nhi balki ek emotion hai.
Ek Saath baithkar popcorn khana,
Baat baat pe papa se apni manpasand team jeetegi iske liye jhagda krna,
Kis waqt kaun baazi maar Jaye uska dar rehna,
Dhoni, jab 3 runs chaiye tab aakhri ball pe sixxer marta hai uski kushi hona,
Bhala koi movie ya serial itne sare emotions ek saath de skta hai ?
Yahi to hai hamara iske liye pyaar.

Asli maza to tab aata tha jab hum gaon me sabhi ke Saath ek parde pe match Dekha krte the.
Haaye!
Yahi to khasiyat hai iss khel ki jo hum sab ko ek Saath jodta hai

Accha Mai to iss Baar Mumbai Indians ki taraf se hu
Aur aap?

Mohit Goyal

He is a banker by profession, writer by passion and Peculiar Indian by choice. He works in Punjab National Bank at day and likes to write at night. He likes to make memes, write poems, quotes and write-ups. To follow him and read more about his work, follow him on Facebook or Instagram. His Username is Peculiarindian.

My First Encounter with Cricket, Then and Now

I was just 8-9 years old when my father introduced me to Cricket. He bought a Cricket Bat for me when I was too young to play, but never found the interest in it. But it was the year 2003, when the saw the match against Namibia on 23 February 2003. What I saw made me wonder what was exactly happening there that the people around me were cheering for them. I remember clearly the master blaster, Sachin Tendulkar and Sourav Ganguly were batting and were dealing in fours and sixes hitting really big sixes.

That was the time when I got so involved in Cricket, I begin watching matches day night... I used to think about it all the time. Then just when I was beginning to like cricket, I watched the innings of Virender Sehwag, his innings of Multan, that's how his nickname came into existence, Sultan of Multan. First Indian to score 300 in Tests. And that was just the beginning. I began to watch all matches religiously.

I got so caught up in cricket, my studies begin to suffer because all the time my mind used to wander around cricket scores, run rates, overs and strike-rate and everything.

With time, I realise what my father said about cricket is really true. It's not just a game anymore its religion for us, Indians. We eat, pray and sleep cricket.

Everyone just knows about IPL and its team. But I was so involved and hooked in Cricket, I used to watch ICL matches, Indian Cricket League, which was succeeded by Indian Premier League.

Since then, we have come a long way, winning T20 World Cup in South Africa in 2007, then winning 50 Overs World

Cup in 2011, and becoming the first team to win world cup at home soil, and winning the Champions Trophy beating England in England in 2013.

I have seen it all, just waiting for the Delhi Capitals, aka Delhi Daredevils win its first IPL title. I wish I see it soon.

Sidharth Supali

Siddharth Supali is post graduate journalism and mass communication student, He is a writer, videographer, photographer, analyser.

Kings XI Punjab

Kings XI Punjab plays in the Indian premier league established in 2008, the franchise is jointly owned by Mohit Burman, Ness Wadia, Preity Zinta and Karan Paul. The team plays its home matches at the PCA stadium, Mohali. Since the 2010 IPL.

In 2007, the Board of control for cricket in India (BCCI) created the cricket tournament the Indian premier league based on the twenty 20 formats of the game. franchises for Kings XI Punjab auction entry bought by the Dabur group's Mohit Burman (46) percentage, the Wadia group's Ness Wadia (23) percentage, Preity Zinta (23) percentage and Saptarshi Dey of the dey group (minor stake).

Team captain K.L Rahul, Director of cricket operations and head coach Anil Kumble, Brand ambassador Preity Zinta, CEO Satish Menon, Team manager Avinash Vaidya, Assistant coach Andy flower, Mentor Chris Gayle, Batting coach Wasim JAFFER, Bowling coach Charl Langeveldt, Fielding coach Jonty Rhodes, Team physio Andrew Leipus, Assistant physiotherapist Abhijit kar, Trainer Adrian Le Roux, Assistant trainer Prabhakar B, Massuer Naresh Kumar, R&D consultant Sankar Rajgopa

Flairs and Glairs, a platform by a student for the students. We are esteemed youth struggling to carve out our path for our future and we follow a basic mindset Since everyone is not born with all-round skills. Joining hands with people who are born to execute it with perfection is the best way to evolve. Self-Evolution is the need of the hour but, evolving as a community is what we strive for. The initiative as kickstarted by, Founder-Mr. Shubham Shah with the motive to utilize the skillset and talent of writing has now a team of 10+ people who are actively participating into newer forms of learning and discovering talents among youngsters. We Provide platform and services like Publishing opportunities, Open mics, Workshops, Hands-on training. Operating with Brand Name Of Flairs and Glairs (Publication House), we offer the chance of elevating a passionate writer to an esteemed author With Brand name Teekhe Zasbaaat, We bring to you an opportunity to get accustomed with the Public Speaking and Presenting of Thoughts along with regular challenges to brush up your inking spirit. The newest initiative to extend our services we introduced in a new writing Platform- The Glittering Fables and Ink Over Tears.

We Choose to Fly Like A Falcon than to be a

Leg Pulling Crab.

www.ingramcontent.com/pod-product-compliance
Ingram Content Group UK Ltd.
Pitfield, Milton Keynes, MK11 3LW, UK
UKHW022004190726
13853UKWH00004B/1726

9 789390 416837